For Alice, Hugh, and Margaret

First American edition 1995 published by
Ticknor & Fields Books for Young Readers
A Houghton Mifflin company, 215 Park Avenue South,
New York, New York 10003.

First published in 1995 by Frances Lincoln Ltd., London, UK

Manufactured in Italy
The text of this book is set in 24 pt. Gill Sans
The illustrations are cut paper reproduced in full color
10 9 8 7 6 5 4 3 2 1

LIBRARY OF CONGRESS CATALOGING-IN-PUBLICATION DATA
Davenport, Zoë.   Garden / by Zoë Davenport.
p. cm. — (Words for everyday) ISBN 0-395-71538-5
1. Gardens—Miscellanea—Juvenile literature.
2. Plants—Miscellanea—Juvenile literature.
3. Garden fauna—Miscellanea—Juvenile literature.
[1. Gardens—Miscellanea. 2. Vocabulary.]
I. Title II.Series: Davenport, Zoë. Words for everyday.
SB457.D38 1995   635—dc20
94-21456   CIP   AC

WORDS FOR EVERYDAY

GARDEN

BY ZOË DAVENPORT

TICKNOR & FIELDS BOOKS FOR YOUNG READERS

NEW YORK 1995

tree

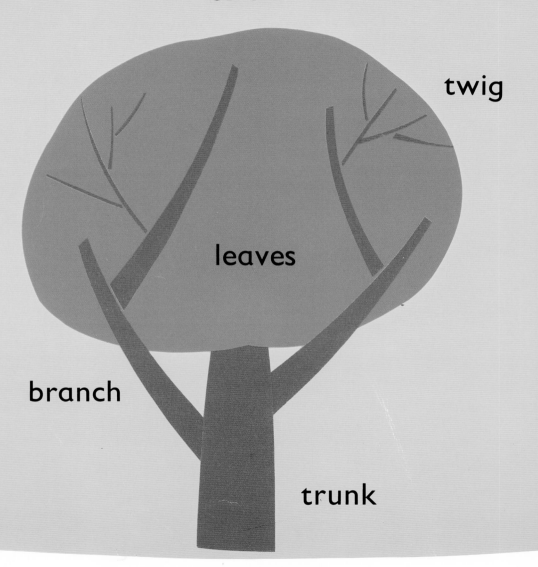

twig

leaves

branch

trunk

ladybug

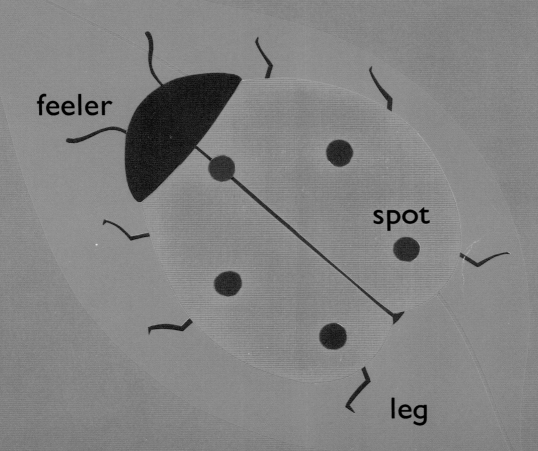

feeler

spot

leg

plant

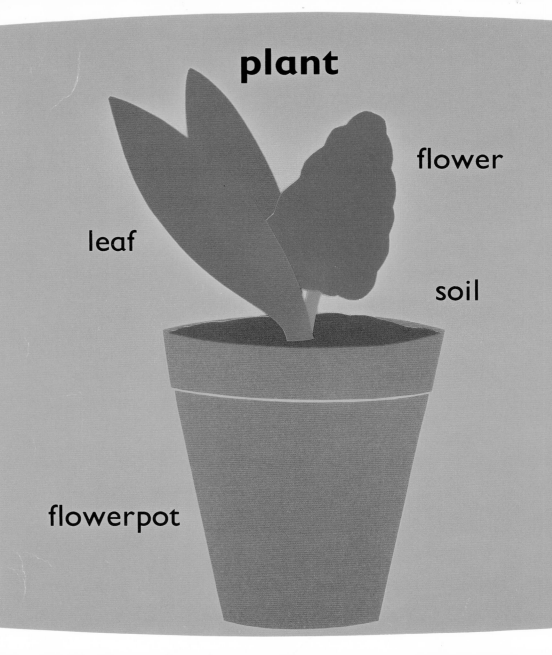

flower

leaf

soil

flowerpot

blackbird

eye

beak

wing

claw

tail

flower

petal

leaf

stem

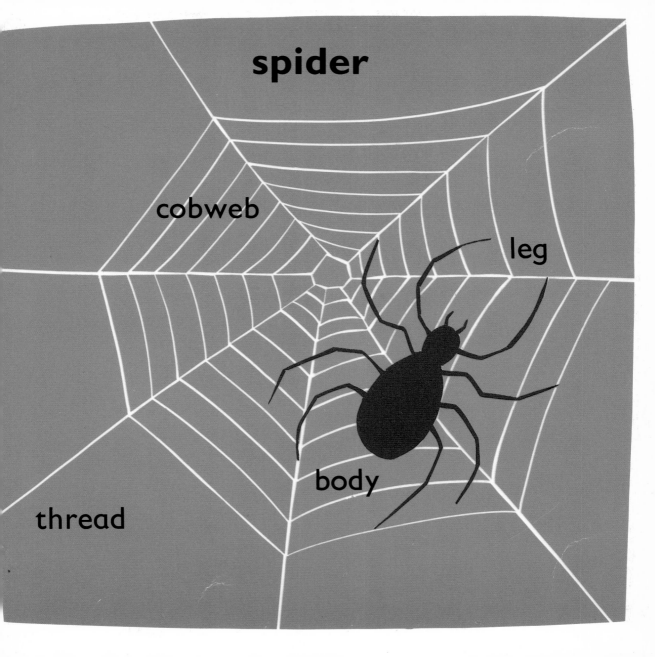

spider

cobweb

leg

body

thread

bird feeder

roof

bird

water

birdseed

pole

watering-can

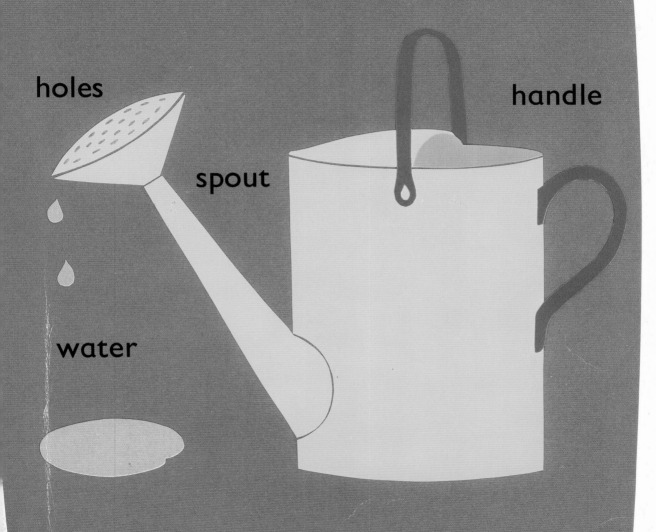

holes

handle

spout

water

MARTIN LUTHER KING JR. BR.

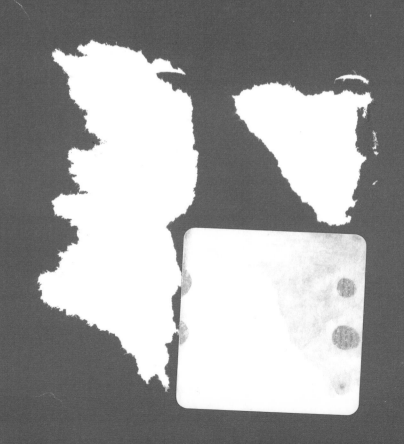